Easter:
McEaster Valley

Easter: McEaster Valley

Walter R. Hoge, DVM

Printed in the United States of America
ISBN 978-1-958434-71-0 (sc)
ISBN 978-1-958434-72-7 (hc)
ISBN 978-1-958434-73-4 (e)

Library of Congress Control Number: 2022922120

2022.12.02

MainSpring Books
5901 W. Century Blvd
Suite 750
Los Angeles, CA, US, 90045

www.mainspringbooks.com

Dreams and aspirations in our lives often are the catalytic events that lead to great accomplishments for the benefit of us and the world in which we live . . .

I dedicate this book to our human family.

May we all remain as youthful with active imagination, hopes, dreams, far sight, and vision for what the world can become. To be always excited about life with full anticipation exuding innocence, warmth, and a bright glowing spirit ready to face the future with courage.

To My **Family**

Many years ago, during the early light of day, I was walking in the Sierra foothills with my Labrador retriever, Beau. As the sun began to rise in the east, I noticed a passageway into a valley that shone like gold, much the same as the sun's reflection appears when it sets at the end of the day and reflects off the windows to the east. I didn't think much about it and continued walking eastward on the south side of the valley entrance.

Approximately twenty minutes later, I again looked toward the valley. The color of gold had changed to the various colors of vegetation, with a beautiful blue cloudless sky marking the horizon. However, the colors were bright and seemed to glow, more like a painting than the familiar California countryside to which I had become accustomed. I also noticed that Beau became more excited as we walked closer and closer to the entrance into the valley. His nose was to the ground, and he circled from side to side in front of me, smelling the ground and pausing from time to time, lifting his head and looking into the direction of the valley. The sides of his chest heaved as he pulled the cool morning air into and out of his nostrils, and his moist tongue was fully out of his mouth as he attempted to taste what he couldn't smell. His muscles quivered; his full attention was directed toward the valley, and I remember thinking how the way he was acting bothered me.

I spent several minutes almost in a trance, looking into the beautiful valley and watching Beau's reactions to things that his sensitive nervous system was picking up while mine was clueless. My first inclination was to turn away from the valley and head back to camp. However, as I looked into the valley, I felt warmth and peace that I can only describe as how I felt as a child when I had hurt myself and my mother held me close to her, assuring me that everything would be okay. I was drawn to the valley as if it had something to offer and if I didn't respond, I would never have another opportunity. My fears and anxieties seemed to melt away as I was drawn to the edge of the valley. I began my descent, following a very small rock- and a brush-covered trail that wound back and forth across the steep hill.

I noticed as I entered the valley that my backpack seemed lighter and my muscles felt stronger and didn't ache. I was beginning to experience the same feelings I had felt as a young child: everything was good and nothing could or would prevent me from being what or whom I wanted to be. With a sense of euphoria, I began running down the trail, throwing down my pack and the other survival equipment I had with me. I was young, I was free from my cares and worries, I was invincible. Physically, I had never felt better. My mind was alive, and I could see and hear and smell and taste and touch and feel things better than I ever had before. This was truly a dream come true. Or was it a dream of heaven? I didn't care. I was treasuring every moment, as every cell of my being was alive and at full alert.

began running, running, and running down the hill with the grace of a deer and the speed of a cheetah, not tiring, not falling, not feeling a care in the world. The trail began to widen, and the ground flattened. I noticed that the trees became taller, and thickets of brush began to close in around the trail. A thorn caught my pant leg as I rounded a corner, and I fell to the ground and rolled until I became embedded in a briar patch. I struggled for several minutes to release myself only to find my clothing torn. I had several bleeding thorn wounds, bruises, and a weakened, shaking, cold body with no first aid kit. I was unable to locate Beau. Retracing my steps, I could not find my way back to the path, and I felt very alone and lost. I remembered what I learned in scouts: use the STOP technique to find my way. S = stop, T = think, O = observe, and P = plan. I had stopped, and I was trying to think.

Everything that I observed was unfamiliar, and none of my plans were working. A way back could not be found, and the farther back I went, the more lost I became.

The only opening in the woods was toward unfamiliar territory, and I could see some light in that direction. I felt desperate, very tired, hungry, scared, and physically exhausted. I thought to ask the Lord for help, but my thoughts and the words coming out of my mouth made me feel so unworthy, I didn't even attempt prayer. I pushed forward with tears of desperation and anger raining down my cheeks. I aimlessly moved through the woods, tearing more clothing, sweating, continuing to cut and bruise my body, dehydrating, getting more hypothermic, and not thinking clearly. I don't remember how many times I became completely exhausted and fell to the earth in a deep sleep. I would awaken seemingly several hours later and then continue the journey, feeling more destitute and depressed than the time before. I vividly remember seeing an open area through the brush and pushing with all the strength I could muster until I escaped onto a green, grassy clearing. I became unconscious, and when I awoke, the sun was coming up again in the east.

As I was gazing into the cloudless sky, a shadow moved over me and I heard a voice say, "We've been waiting for you. You have been chosen to come to our valley." I turned my head towards the voice and saw a longhaired, bearded man about five feet tall with a reassuring, partially toothless smile. He had a long nose that was widened at the base. His entire face was furrowed with age, and he seemed to keep his right eye nearly closed as if trying to focus. His left eye was wide open and reminded me of a cat's eye when it is concentrating on prey. His arms and legs seemed short because he had large feet and a grandpa's belly with a wide belt that seemed to be overstretched. The clothes he wore were clean and neat and of earth tones that seemed to blend into the wooded background. He reminded me of the trolls that inhabit the mountains and forests of Norway.

He helped me up, commenting on the condition of my body and soul, and told me that he was taking me home to get cleaned up and to get some food in my stomach. As we walked along a path, I couldn't help but notice the beautiful countryside. Everything seemed to be bright and have the glow I noticed when standing at the rim of the valley. I also noticed that the trail we were on, as well as the pathways leading from it, was clean of rocks and debris, and the ground consisted of a firmly packed clay-like material that looked well-traveled.

Here and there, I noticed large fur-covered footprints that had been placed there by an animal, the looks of which I couldn't imagine. I immediately thought of Big Foot of the Southwest, but these were not primate feet. I couldn't help notice how quick of wit this old man seemed to be. He anticipated what I was going to say, and everything seemed exciting and fun. He didn't at all act his age. I couldn't help but notice that when I made remarks about how I was feeling and the struggle it was walking down the trail, he always had something positive to say. He walked fast, stopped from time to time to look at things of interest, and shared his enthusiasm and knowledge of the flora and fauna in the area. I couldn't help but have my spirits lifted by just being with him. Here I was, a fairly young man (compared to him) of reason-able intelligence and in fairly good physical condition being out walked, out talked, and uplifted by a man who I should be pushing in a wheelchair and feeding with a straw.

In the distance, I could see two large and very tall redwood-like conifers that seemed to stand one on each side of the path upon which we were traveling.

Just beyond the trees, it looked like the trail ended abruptly at the base of a mountain. As we got closer to the trees, I noticed that the trail did not end but began sloping down into the ground. At this time, my new friend encouraged me on and commented that as we passed the trees, we would be going into the main area of the valley where he lived. The entrance into the mountain was wide and high enough to accommodate the passage of several large men walking abreast of each other and the path sloped gently down into the mountain. As the light of the entrance faded behind us, I noticed that all along the tunnel wall, there was a light greenish glow that increased in intensity as the area around us darkened.

My first thought was that the glowing light looked like radium, which used to be used on the hands of wristwatches to help them glow in the dark. A touch of fear struck me as I thought about radium and the radiation that it emits as it excites phosphorus to produce the light. Marie Curie extracted radium from pitchblende in the early twentieth century and eventually died from the effects of radiation overexposure from the concentrated element. I also noticed that the underground air did not have that stale, moldy, moist smell, and the temperature remained comfortable. The air was dry and had a pleasant before-the-storm smell to it.

I noticed that the deeper we traveled, the warmer the ground and walls of the tunnel became. I again became a little concerned, because the warmer ground could mean that we were getting farther into the earth, near the magma layer, where all the molten rock can be found. I also knew that the earth's core is kept very hot due in part to radioactive decay. If I were getting radiation exposure from radium in the tunnel and the molten rocks below, I might end up like Marie Curie, which would not be a nice way to go.

After about an hour of walking in the tunnel, the ground began to level and the opening widened.

In the distance, I could see light from the end of the tunnel, and when we emerged, the light was as intense as the sun and the landscape reminded me of what I had seen while looking into the valley with Beau. Within a short time, we took a path to the left and then the third path to the right. We continued straight ahead until we came upon a house that reminded me of an old eighteenth-century European farmhouse. However, I could only see a front because the home was built straight into the mountainside.

efore we could reach the front porch, the door opened and there appeared a female version of my friend. The only way I can describe her is that she was very much like the perfect wife, the perfect mother, and the perfect grandmother all wrapped up into one. As she greeted us, you could see and feel the love that she had for her husband, and I knew that her concern over my well-being was heartfelt and sincere. She also seemed to have endless energy. While my friend helped bathe and clean me, she immediately began preparing the best smelling (and I might add tasting) meal I could ever remember. Over the years, I have often remembered that meal. At first, I thought it was so special because at the time I was so tired and in such need of nourishment. However, I have had many opportunities since that time to be very tired and very hungry and sit down to a meal prepared by some of the best trained in culinary skills. I can honestly tell you that since that meal, I have never again had such food. What gets me is that I watched her prepare that meal using only what looked like simple plant materials and no seasoning. After I ate, she reached into the cupboard and opened a vial of what looked like oil and had a musky smell. She placed it into her aged hands, rubbed them together, and placed the material on my sores. Her hands were thin and wrinkled, with aging spots; but when she placed them on my skin, they felt warm and soft, and I could feel the strength in her hands as she massaged my body. Wherever she massaged my skin, it began to heal, and the soreness and tiredness of my body seemed to melt away. It felt so warm and so relaxing. It felt supernatural, maybe even spiritual.

The rest of that evening can only be described as warm, friendly, caring, and loving, and my mind and soul were overpowered with peace and joy. I was truly in a state of ecstasy. The warm night clothing and the bed I was given for the evening sent me into a deep, most restful sleep.

The next morning, I awakened, instantly alert. My mind seemed alive, and my body felt in its prime, just as it had when I entered the valley. My mind took in all that was going on around me, and I seemed to anticipate things before they happened (as my friend had). As I sat up in bed, there was a quiet knock at the door, and my friend spoke a good morning greeting to me through the door. I was shown where to take care of my personal needs and instructed when breakfast would be served.

During the morning meal, I asked about the strange things I had noticed and felt since I had entered the valley. He answered my questions directly and with honesty. There were many things told to me that I would not have understood if my mind had not been as alert and in a different state than it was accustomed to. He also stated again that I had been chosen to come to the valley but gave no further explanation. He told me that the valley had been prepared with the intent that no one could enter unless they were invited. Its sole purpose was to provide service to the peoples of the world and those who stayed dedicated themselves, to receive, only from within, any rewards for their eternal effort.

An electric jolt went through my spine when he used the word eternal. I repeated his word: "Eternal?"

Matter-of-factly, he said, "Yes, eternal. You see my wife's and my body and what do you see?" Without waiting for an answer, he continued, "What you see are older people whose bodies look withered and useless. I think I noted your thoughts yesterday when the words wheelchair and being fed by a straw entered your mind." I was embarrassed but I also was convinced at this time that he could know anything and, for that matter, do anything he wanted. "My wife and I entered this valley many years ago. During our stay, the physical outer self has changed but the mind, body, and soul have become heightened to its maximum capacity. We're not superhuman. We are humans who have reached the maximum capacity in all that we are. We are the best we can be, not only in our mind, body, and soul but also in our relationship with each other and those who reside in the valley surrounding us. I have always looked at it as the way our God pictured how life on the rest of this earth could be if everyone would just put their minds to it. Our mission is to try to help those on planet earth direct their attention, at least one day a year, toward their creator and what he has done for us.

We accomplish this task by doing caring and fun things in such a way that everyone can participate.

Their attention may be toward nature and its gift of life, or towards the savior and his giving of his life for us so that we may have the gift of life. Or their attention may just be placed towards the family having a fun-filled day with hidden gifts, candy, and toys." Then he paused for a moment and repeated the word eternal. "Yes, by living in this valley and serving the citizens of the world, we do not die. I will always be as you see me this day. I may not be much to look at, but remember, I am the best I can be and will always be this way." He then ended our conversion, saying it was time for me to be given a tour of the valley.

We walked out the back door of his home and were on our way. I was a little confused because when we entered his home through the front door the day before, I noticed that the house was built into the mountainside. He told me that since I was a guest, there were only certain areas of the valley I could visit and not all my questions could be answered. The area we were walking through could best be described as a rural country with thickets and forests scattered throughout the region. The moist vegetation looked succulent and very green, giving the appearance of early spring. I noticed that there were storm clouds and an occasional lightning bolt off in the distance. Flowers of all kinds and colors could be found carpeting the ground and in many of the trees. The grassy areas reminded me of the beautiful flowers I had seen in my youth, growing up the mountainsides of Idaho in the spring as the snow slowly melted towards the tops of the mountains.

I just stood there awed by the sights, sounds, and smells of the area. I experienced a feeling of being young and clean and, for lack of a better word, reborn. There seemed to be lots and lots of young animals everywhere. There were proportionately more chicks, ducklings, and bunnies than adults, and they seemed to be very friendly and wanted me to hold and pet them. My friend casually mentioned it was hard to produce enough of these young animals because the demand was increasing faster than the valley could supply them. I had a strong feeling that I shouldn't ask him why, at least at this time. I made a mental note to later do so as we continued our walk through the area.

We crossed a clear stream and started walking towards its tributaries. Where two creeks entered the stream, we turned down a path away from the flowing water. Several minutes later, we approached and entered a doorway that went into the base of a tree. My friend mentioned that because of my medical background, he wanted to show me something of interest. We walked into a very clean and neatly kept room. I immediately recognized the smell of chickens. Many years ago during my college days in Indiana, a poultry class I was taking visited a chicken farm that smelled about the same. We were learning about the industry–the feeding of the chickens, rearing of young pullets for egg production, care of the eggs produced, and what happens to an old hen, which is called a spent hen.

He went back into a cool storage room, which I think was an area carved out in the tree, and produced an egg. This egg was perfect in shape and appeared not to be spoiled. The only defect I could find was that there were speckles all over the surface. I was told that these eggs were available in everything from a near purple to white and that the color of the speckles could be varied about the same. I thought the eggs were very pretty, and my friend agreed with pride.

THIS PLAQUE IS PRESENTED
IN HONOR OF DR. JONES
FROM THE CENTER OF DISEASE
CONTROL FOR HIS TIRELESS
DEDICATION IN ERADICATING
THE CHICKEN POX

However, with a thoughtful look, he said, "When these speckles first appeared, they almost ruined the egg industry for the valley. In the past, the farmers were very proud of their solid-colored eggs. They were able to produce thick, strong-shelled eggs with solid, even colors that were in high demand. Then one year, about half the chickens became ill. Their egg production dropped, and the eggs produced were of different sizes and shapes.

A lot of these eggs were also speckled. With only about half the eggs normally produced available and demand high, no one knew what to do.

"We then arranged to have some specialists brought into the valley to examine our chickens and their eggs. They came here in much the same way you appeared yesterday. A research doctor whose last name was Jones, from the Center for Disease Control in Atlanta, Georgia, was very helpful. He diagnosed the chickens to have come down with the disease chickenpox. He told us that this form of the disease could not be spread to man and that the eggs were perfectly safe to eat. With the lack of eggs to take their place, we went ahead and distributed the eggs that year. We were embarrassed about those eggs, but much to our surprise, the people were delighted with them and wanted more the next year. We called Dr. Jones back to the valley, and he developed a strain of chickenpox virus that would continue to produce the speckled eggs without making the hens ill." He then led me into a large room where the eggs produced were stored.

There was almost every size and color you could imagine. They had even developed many different shapes of speckles that could be produced by the hens. Thoughts of line breeding, cross-breeding, and inbreeding flowed through my mind, and I could only imagine the genetic combinations along with the viral components that could produce such an array of eggs. I was oh so desirous to see more but was advised that, as a visitor, this was all I was allowed to see.

We walked out of the same door that we had entered. I was dragging my feet but encouraged that other things to be seen would also be exciting.

While walking down the trail, my friend mentioned that there was a lot of demand for food at one particular time of the year. The demand could only be met by producing food year-round. The food items most in demand were chocolate and hard candy, plus soft, animal-shaped marshmallow treats. Many years ago, even though there were fewer people on the earth, there were never enough of these items available during the season when demand was high. He said that much of the food would spoil if it were stored for several weeks. Then, with a wink from his most always wide-opened eye, he said, "Let me show you the technique we've found to store food for not only several weeks but several years." We traveled into a darker part of the trail. Vines were growing above us and some large gourd-shaped fruit or vegetables clinging to the vines. I mentioned these and was told that they were vegetables and had been developed as a food source for the insects that produced the main ingredient for the food storage process. He stated that as they increased the size of the insects, they also had to find a plentiful, highly productive plant to feed them. The plant was able to do very well on some of the less productive ground that was near a warmer region of the valley.

The increased warmth stimulated the insects to grow rapidly and produce the "milk," as he called it, to add as a preservative to the food products being made. I was told that the insects resembled aphids and the "milk" they secreted from their bodies was a complex carbohydrate (sugar). This sugar is much like the sweet material produced by normal aphids that honeydew ants harvest for their food. The milk was collected during the cleaning process of the pens in which they were kept. I was told directly that I could not visit the aphid pens. However, he did allow me to go a little out of our way and see the large bees (not honey bees) that they had developed to make a special, very thin honeycomb, which was used in the storage process. I politely declined. Having allergies, I wasn't sure taking a chance of finding large, allergenic, pollen-producing plants or toxic stingers had any potential of improving the great day I was having. He seemed a little disappointed but quickly recovered and informed me that after we took a short rest, we were at least going to see what they had developed to perform the final task in the food storage process. I agreed without daring to ask for further information.

I rested, and he spent the time enthusiastically answering questions and pointing to things he did not want me to miss. We then continued deeper along the darkened trail, and the path became more and more covered with moist leaves and debris. We had to watch our footing, and I almost stepped on a large, slimy banana slug as we entered what looked like a cave opening covered by a porous netting.

Inside it smelled moist and like a potato cellar, and towards the rear of the cave, there was a dark glow penetrating the darkness. On either side of the cave, there were boxes filled with what looked like soil containing wormlike glowing larvae, and at the end of the cave, glowing insects were flying inside a cage. I commented that these looked like glow worms and fireflies. My friend said that this was correct but had me notice that the light emitted was a different brightness and cautioned me to not get too close or the corneas of my eyes may be damaged. The light emitted from the insects caused some of my clothing to give off a greenish glow similar to that seen in a spook alley lit with black lights. He told me that the light these valuable insects were giving off had been developed to change the surface of food and form a thin airtight seal that would protect it from spoiling for years. When the food came in contact with water of any kind, the seal would dissolve away and not harm those eating it. He then informed me that our next stop would be the food preservation area.

We walked to the back of the cave and through a door, into a brightly lit white room. On one wall, I could see stainless steel countertops and a conveyer belt that entered through the wall. I was told that on the other side of the wall was where the food was prepared, and this side of the wall was where the food was preserved. He said that the milk produced by the aphid-like insects was mixed into the food before cooking. After the food passed from the other side of the wall into the preservation room, a very thin, honeycomb, waxy material (from the bees) was placed under and on top of the food.

The food was then rolled on the conveyer belt to a covered chamber on the other side of the room, which contained the adult fireflies. The food would pass through this chamber in about four and a half seconds and then pass out through the wall behind the chamber. It was then placed deep within the mountain, near the tunnel I passed through the day before. This area was very warm and dry, which was necessary to keep the food fresh. My friend mentioned that if I decided to stay, I would be quite involved with this part of the valley's activities. I caught the words decide to stay and planned to ask what he meant when we returned to his home. We stayed in this area and had a very good lunch. I only wish they had been in production during our visit.

However, I was quite certain that I was taken to this area so I would not get to see what was going on.

After lunch, I was told that we were getting away from living and going into the area of toy production. Since I worked with animals, I was a little disappointed, but I knew whatever he showed me would be of interest.

A short distance from the food preservation area, we climbed a spiral staircase that was cut into the bark of a large tree. We must have gone up about forty feet when we reached a ledge with a basket hooked onto a vine-like something from Tarzan. I couldn't see where it went but it seemed to gradually slope down towards the ground. My friend jumped inside the basket and eased my shaking body inside.

The basket was untied from the tree, and away we went. I didn't see much. The only thing I could think to do was hang on with all my might and look into the basket. However, I did notice two things in the direction we were headed that did not make sense.

The sun was very bright, and I saw several large rainbows in the area. The vine cable ended near the front door of a large building. The roof went up on all four sides and formed a large, circle. I couldn't tell if the circular structure was open or covered. My hand was grabbed and I was briskly pulled towards the building while being told that I could figure it out when I got inside.

The building was large inside, and for the first time, I saw other people who were living in the valley. They looked very happy and moved briskly as they worked. They were all colors, shapes, and sizes, and most looked old like my friend and his wife. In the center of the building, from the ceiling down, was a large structure that looked like a funnel. The large rim attached to the ceiling had a diameter about the same distance across as the circle I had seen on the roof. At the bottom of the funnel, several hoses were coming out from the circular rim. They came to a point on the end, with a bright light shining through. Several workers were carefully holding these tubes, and it looked like they were tracing or drawing. I was amazed at the speed and accuracy of the work. However, I had no idea what they were doing. My friend, anticipating my thoughts, told me that in this building they were cutting out materials for making toys. He went on to tell me that the large coned area on the roof was used to trap the sun's rays. It had been built in the valley where the sun shined the most throughout the year, and there were several buildings like this one in the area. They had developed cells within the cone that intensified the sun's energy and created an intensified light that cut through the material, similar to laser technology. However, the technology was simple and the cones were also used for heating and lighting if other energy sources were not available (i.e. the light and warmth I had found in the tunnel). I was told not to talk to the workers, but I watched for several minutes as they used one area to cut material and others to stitch or weld the pieces together. I recognized many of the toys, and what was going on in the valley seemed to make more sense.

It was called to my attention that it was getting late, so I followed my escort along a walkway to the other end of the building. We took some stairs down into a tunnel, walked away, and went back up some stairs into another building. This building was also painted white inside. However, when we walked through two large doors, I could see that the opposite wall was multi-colored. As I looked more closely, I could see streaks of color coming from the ceiling and painted down the wall. There were also many workers present, and it looked like they were painting. As we walked closer, I realized the streaks of color were not painted on the wall but radiating from the ceiling down, and there were small waterfalls in the building, creating a mist that lingered throughout the colors. Several large trees looked like palms with very smooth trunks; they had faucet like structures embedded in them. I was close enough to watch the workers. They would come over to the trees with an empty bucket, open the faucet, and collect a small amount of liquid. Then they would go over to the colored streaks and place the bucket under an area of the color they wanted. As long as the bucket was in the mist and under the desired color, the bucket would fill with paint. I studied the color streaks very carefully.

Something was beginning to ring a bell, to ring a bell. First of all, I noticed that the colors seemed to come right through the roof from the sky above. Second, the colors bled from one color into the next and a worker had available almost any color he wanted. In astonishment, I said what it was: "Workers can get any of the colors found in the rainbow." That was it! Or was it? I asked my friend, and he just looked at me and said nothing.

He did tell me though that the paint was non-toxic and could be made to be permanent or removed easily. To paint edible items in the next building, they used a slightly different version of the same paint.

My friend again stressed that it was getting late, and when we opened the large doors and stepped outside, it was pitch black.

As my eyes adjusted to the darkness, I began to see tiny lights everywhere. I rubbed my eyes, and yes, it was true. The entire area was dimly lit by thousands of illuminating insects found everywhere in the grass, air, and shrubbery. At this point, I didn't even ask about the insects. The entire day was so awesome and unnatural that I had begun accepting everything as natural. Everything had been so beautiful and perfect and stimulating. How could I have been so lucky to stumble into this paradise so close to home?

We walked at a brisk pace and soon found ourselves back at his home, having another meal to be remembered. It was not long before I felt the same warmth, joy, and peace that felt so good the night before. My friend's wife seemed a little more hurried as she tidied things up after we helped with the dishes. She excused herself and, I assume, went to bed. We had a visit that is as vivid today as it was then. He politely answered a few of my questions and then began what I would call a real soul talk with me. I say this because everything said between us seemed to come from the heart and between two friends who had known each other for a long time. It was if I were in a more perfect state and that normal daily emotions such as fear, anxiety, aggression, pride, lust, anger, etc., had never been a part of my life.

He began by telling me that I had not stumbled into their valley. The residents had spent a long time choosing me. They wanted me to stay and dedicate my talents to their cause, and the only reward I could expect was the feeling one has when he gives service without recognition. If I came, it would be permanent; I would not taste death. I would look aged on the outside but eternally young in mind, body, and soul. I was educated in a profession that they needed, and I seemed to love my work and had been consistent in my ethics. I had not shown any signs of growing up. I seemed to sing and dance and play my days away regularly, and my downs didn't seem to last long. I seemed to be tolerant of others and usually didn't get in the way of the creativity or contributions they made. He then looked me straight in the eye and said that I could sleep on it but my decision needed to be made before the sun rose the next morning. We shook hands and gave each other a big hug. My eyes became moist, and I thought I could see a tear or two in the corner of his large left eye.

I placed the same warm night clothing on and slipped into the same bed that I had slept in the evening before. I even fell into a deep sleep, but this time I was vividly aware of my dreams and I tossed over and over as my mind pondered what I should do. I felt my wife and young children needed my presence to have a better chance of experiencing normal, healthy lives. I knew that money would not be an issue since, after some time, I would be declared dead and there was plenty of insurance to take care of their needs. I was very attracted to the new and exciting things that I could learn if I stayed. My mind pondered over the large fur-covered footprint, the giant aphids, the sap from the trees that extracted color from the rainbow, feeling young and strong forever, having an alert mind that could quickly do so many things, rubbing shoulders with people who have reached the maximum capacities of who they could be and experiencing the love that radiated from their relationships. The list could go on and on. The last thing I remember before falling into unconsciousness sleep was feeling the need to see my family and the things that had made my life worthwhile.

Something wet on the side of my neck and face aroused me, but my mind was dull and I couldn't seem to wake up. I also noticed that every muscle ached and I felt like I had been laying on a rock.

When I finally focused my eyes, there was a large head peering straight into my face. I pulled my head back a little and could see the moist pink tongue and black-haired face of my dog, Beau. I lay there for several minutes, confused as to where I was or what had happened to me. I looked at my watch and it was three hours later than when I remembered last looking for the time.

slowly rose to my feet and looked towards the valley I thought I had visited. The valley was there, but its colors were not any brighter or showing more of a painted glow than the surrounding Sierra foothills. I wondered if this were all a dream. It couldn't be. There were too many vivid experiences and too many things I saw that I could not have created or imagined in a three-hour dream. I was too tired to give the valley another look and turned away to slowly head back to camp.

Years later when my children were young, they used to lay on my bed with me and I would tell them stories. I would always start with the words "A long, long, long time ago in a land far, far, far away..." in hopes that they would fall asleep before I would have to make up a story. When my mind could not create new adventures, I would fall back on the experiences I had in the valley a long time before. My children seemed to like these stories the best. They expressed to me that they were more believable and I never changed the stories. I named the valley McEaster Valley, and the friend I had there, Mr.

McEaster. It was obvious to me that I had been allowed to help the people of the world celebrate Easter. Every Easter morning, I would get up to evaluate the toys, candy, and eggs to see what improvements had been made since my visit. New things showed up from time to time, and I tried to imagine what had happened in McEaster Valley to stimulate the change.

Since visiting McEaster Valley, I have taken the supposed problems of the world a little less seriously. We are constantly striving to make our lives simpler but are, in reality, making them more complicated. When the push and stress get to be too much for me, I think of McEaster Valley and the order of nature and the innocent animals living their lives and accepting whatever comes their way by putting their best foot forward and going on. Most of us don't seem to realize that God made this earth and placed us on it so we could have joy and learn who we are before going on to the next estate. When I hear that the world is becoming hotter because of the burning of fossil and other fuels and that the ice caps will melt, leaving cities underwater and causing severe climate changes, I think of McEaster Valley. I remember how nature in balance was used to provide heat, light, and energy to produce things the people needed. When I observe the terrible things governments and people do to each other, I know that it can be different as I recall the people of McEaster Valley and the beautiful relationships they had one with another. When I see myself or others with unhealthy bodies, I think of the healing capacities of the musky-smelling oil that healed my body. I know from my visit to McEaster Valley that we make things too hard as we go through our lives.

We have too many "what ifs" that never happen, and we don't set all our fears and anxieties aside as "so what's" until they become problems that need to be dealt with.

I have now reached the point in my life where my children have a pretty much-left home and they are taking good care of themselves. I also recently became unexpectedly alone. I've found that as the family grows, the parents find themselves needed more and more for the care and well-being of their children. Then suddenly, their family is gone and they begin to feel unneeded. You still have something to contribute, but no one seems to be reaching out in need. I have recently been finding myself thinking more and more about McEaster Valley and the opportunities there were to contribute my time and talents towards a good cause. I wonder if there was only one chance to accept an offer to live there. I would sure like to have some of that musky smelling oil to rub on my sore ankle and back. And, of course, I would like to again be able to run like the wind and feel, as a youth, that all is good and nothing can or will prevent me from being what or whom I want to be.

I now have a new young Labrador retriever by the name of Maui. This one is yellow and a female who has had extensive training to develop her nose. She returns if I whistle two times, and she can go and go all day. Just maybe I can find again the spot in the Sierra foothills where I found McEaster Valley. Just maybe Maui could pick up the scent Beau smelled so many years ago. Just maybe my ankle and back could make the climb. Just maybe I'll try again. But for now, I'll take a power nap before formalizing my plans.

**Easter: McEaster Valley
by Walter R. Hoge**

Rating: **Gold**

Easter: McEaster Valley is a unique and fascinating story of a man who underwent a life-changing experience in the woods

In this delightful book, author Walter R. Hoge shares how a walk in the woods changed his life and his views of it forever. Walking in the Sierra foothills one fine day with his dog Beau, Hoge noticed a passageway into a valley that shone like gold. As he and Beau walked closer to the valley, he felt warmth and peace that he could only compare to his mother's comfort. As he got more drawn to the valley, he began his descent but unfortunately fell. Beau is nowhere near him.

Wounded and on the verge of hypothermia, he fell asleep from the exhaustion. Waking up the next morning, he was greeted by an old, bearded man who said they have been waiting for him, and that he was chosen to come to their valley. Spending days in the valley, he discovered things he never knew existed. He was struck by the wonders and mystery of it all.

With a vivid description of the things he saw and experienced, Hoge's book elicits excitement and fascination from the readers. Whether everything he experienced was a dream or not, the book gives us something to think about. While this may be a cliché, the book reminds us that not everything is about money and earthly possessions. Hoge encourages and motivates readers to respect the wonders of the earth and live a life of responsibility without expecting anything in return.

Credit should be given to Hoge for not dismissing everything he saw as absurd and unbelievable. He was accepting and open to the fact that some of the innovations would be useful and would benefit all. This book may be targeted to children, but adults can also learn a lot from this story.

Overall, ***Easter: McEaster Valley*** is a fun and enjoyable read. Aside from the wonderful story, the illustration and the colors add appeal to this well-written book.

Easter: McEaster Valley
by Walter R. Hoge, DVM
ReadersMagnet

Book review by Mark Heisey

"I was drawn to the valley as if it had something to offer and if I didn't respond, I would never have another opportunity."

One early morning, the protagonist and his Labrador retriever took a walk in the Sierra foothills. He noticed an entrance into a beautifully lit valley. As he began traveling on the trail into the valley, he felt all his burdens lift and felt young and carefree. However, at some point, the path started to close in on him, and he was tripped up and rolled into a briar patch. Once free from the briars, he realized he was lost and could not locate his dog. The only direction he could go was forward. After many hours and several long naps, he escaped into an opening and was greeted by a reassuring bearded man. The man took him into a mountain cave that eventually opened and was lit as fantastically as the golden valley he had seen earlier. Here he encountered many people and animals living harmoniously and crafting candies and toys to give out once a year on a special day. The man made him a one-time offer to live there forever, always full of vitality and peace, and help take care of the animals. The man tossed and turned all night, thinking of the opportunity but also about his wife and young children. When he awoke, he was back where he was walking, and his Labrador was licking his face.

Hoge's magical valley is the Easter version of Santa's North Pole. Much of the tale is inspired by those Christmas books and television specials which give glimpses into the business of the elves but with a Spring-inspired point of view. There are moments where Hoge's writing takes on a near-nonfiction tone reminiscent of the holiday classics made popular by Gail Gibbons. Hoge brings his more scientific approach to keeping all those delicious chocolates and other candies fresh and depicts an interesting rainbow-infused paint supply available to the toymakers and confectioners. Speaking of colors, the book includes several bold illustrations by Jebb Impok, which capture some of the delight and whimsy of Easter Valley and its offerings. In a bit of a reflective conclusion, the author engages the audience by speaking of the character's loneliness once his kids have grown and moved away. He also wonders if he can find a way to revisit McEaster Valley.

Hoge's writing is easy to follow, and the descriptions are done well without being excessive. Because of its length and often highly technical phrasing, it is difficult to determine the book's exact audience. Passages such as "Thoughts of line breeding, cross-breeding, and inbreeding flowed through my mind, and I could only imagine the genetic combinations along with the viral components that could produce such an array of eggs" may prove to be too much for younger readers or listeners. Still, parents can obviously use the story and illustrations as the framework for spinning their own yarn about this magical place, adding more of the technical text as their children mature and are capable of discussions. Additionally, it gives them another story option to share when focusing on the more whimsical parts of Easter.